Kingfisher Books, Grisewood & Dempsey Ltd,
Elsley House, 24–30 Great Titchfield Street,
London W1P 7AD

First published in paperback in 1992 by Kingfisher Books
10 9 8 7 6 5 4 3 2 1
Originally published in hardback in 1990 by Kingfisher Books

BRITISH LIBRARY CATALOGUING-IN-PUBLICATION DATA
A catalogue record for this book is available
from the British Library

ISBN: 0 86272 882 7

Phototypeset by Wyvern Typesetting Ltd, Bristol
Colour separations by Newsele Litho, Milan, London
Printed in Hong Kong

Two Tiny Mice

Alan Baker

Kingfisher Books

Two tiny
harvest mice,
what do
they see?

The soft,
furry
rabbit
dozing in
the sun,

the mad March hare,

and the shuffling, snuffling mole,

the shy,
little
hedge
sparrow
in its
nest of
twigs,

the sly
old fox,
high upon
the hill.

Two tiny
harvest mice,
what do
they see?

the croaking frog,

the quacking duck,

the weasel,
on the
river bank,

and the
muddy-brown
otter,
swimming
in the water.

Two tiny
harvest mice,
what do
they see?

The
bright-eyed,
grey squirrel
nibbling on
a nut,

the spiky,
spiny hedgehog,
rustling through
the leaves.

But
do they see
the badgers,
playing
in the dark?

NO . . .

Two tiny harvest mice are home
and sound asleep.